An Animal Friends Reader

by Liza Charlesworth
illustrated by Ian Smith

Text copyright © 2015 by Liza Charlesworth
Illustrations copyright © 2015 Scholastic Inc.

All rights reserved. Published by Scholastic Inc., *Publishers since 1920*. SCHOLASTIC and associated logos are trademarks and/or registered trademarks of Scholastic Inc.

The publisher does not have any control over and does not assume any responsibility for author or third-party websites or their content.

No part of this publication may be reproduced, stored in a retrieval system, or transmitted in any form or by any means, electronic, mechanical, photocopying, recording, or otherwise, without written permission of the publisher. For information regarding permission, write to Scholastic Inc., Attention: Permissions Department, 557 Broadway, New York, NY 10012.

This book is a work of fiction. Names, characters, places, and incidents are either the product of the author's imagination or are used fictitiously, and any resemblance to actual persons, living or dead, business establishments, events, or locales is entirely coincidental.

ISBN: 978-0-545-85963-9

10 9 8 7 6 5 4 3 2   18 19 20 21 22/0

Printed in Malaysia
First printing 2015

106

Book design by Maria Mercado

SCHOLASTIC INC.

The fish read.

The fish write.

The fish count.

The fish build.

The fish eat.

The fish play.

The fish paint.

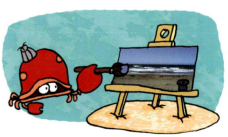

The fish dress up.

The fish love their school!

Comprehension Boosters

1. How is the fish school like a child's school? How is it different?

2. Find the page where the fish count. What are the fish counting?

3. The fish do lots of activities in their school. Which is your favorite? Why?